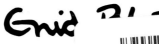

BIBL

The Baby in the Bulrushes

ILLUSTRATED BY STEPHANIE McFETRIDGE BRITT

HARVEST HOUSE PUBLISHERS
Eugene, Oregon 97402

The Baby in the Bulrushes

The children of Israel were living in a strange land—the land of Egypt. They were quite different from the Egyptians around them. They had different ways, and they prayed to a different God.

There came a new King, a Pharaoh who did not like the Children of Jacob—or Children of Israel, as they were now called. He saw that these strangers were becoming very rich and powerful. He spoke to his chief men about them.

3

"What shall we do with these 'Children of Israel?'" he said. "They overrun our land, and maybe when we go to war, these men will join our enemies and fight us."

"What are your commands, lord?" asked the chief men.

"We will make them into slaves," said Pharaoh. "They shall build me treasure-houses; they shall make roads and dig canals."

So masters were put over the Children of Israel, and they were made to work very hard.

They made bricks from the river clay. They put chopped straw with the clay to bind it together, and then the hot sun baked the bricks.

The Egyptian masters beat them cruelly, forcing them to work harder and harder. But still it seemed as if the Children of Israel became greater in numbers.

Pharaoh saw the great number of the Israelites, the Children of Israel, and he gave a terrible command.

"Take every boy baby from its mother, and throw it into the river Nile," he said. "Then there will be no more young Israelite boys growing up."

The women wept bitterly when their little baby boys were taken away and thrown into the river.

There was one mother called Jochabed. She had a beautiful baby son, and she was afraid that the Egyptians would come and take him away. She had another boy, Aaron, and a little daughter Miriam. They were safe—but how could she save her baby boy?

At first she hid him in her house. But as he grew, he cried very loudly, and Jochabed was afraid that a passing Egyptian might hear him.

So she thought of a plan. She said to Miriam, "We will make a little ark out of the bulrushes. Then we will put it among the reeds, near the place where the Egyptian princess comes to bathe each morning."

Miriam and her mother set to work to make the little ark. "It must be just the right size for our baby," said his mother. "We will weave a lid for the ark too, so that the sun will not beat down on his dear little face."

They made a strong little basket.

"Now we will seal it with slime and pitch," said Jochabed. "Then no water will get through the cracks and sink the little ark."

They sealed it well and set it out in the hot sun to dry. When it was quite dry and watertight, they lined it with soft blankets. It was a dear little ark when they had finished.

"Now we will put our baby in it," said Jochabed, and she lifted the child and laid him gently into the ark.

When he was asleep, they slipped down to the water, waiting until there was no one to see them.

"Here are some reeds," said Miriam. "Let us put him there. He will be well hidden."

They set the ark on the waters, and it floated beautifully.

Jochabed lifted up the lid and took a last look at the sleeping child. "Goodbye, my little one," she said, and the tears streamed down her face. She turned to go, and then spoke to Miriam. "Miriam," she said. "Hide yourself away somewhere in sight of the ark. Watch to see what happens to our poor little baby."

The Kind Princess

So Miriam hid herself, and watched the little floating ark. What would happen to their precious baby?

The baby slept peacefully. He did not wake, and he did not cry.

At last Miriam heard voices. She peeped from her hiding place and saw the beautiful Princess of Egypt coming down to bathe in the river. Her maids were with her, and they were all talking and laughing together.

"Go, walk by the river," said the Princess to her maids. "I need only one of you to help me undress."

The Princess began to take off her clothes. She saw the reeds waving in the wind—and then her quick eyes caught sight of something strange in the reeds.

"What is that?" she wondered. "It looks like a little boat made of rushes."

"Shall I go and see?" asked her maid.

"Fetch it for me," said the Princess.

The maid ran to the water. She lifted up the basket and took it to the Princess.

The Princess lifted the lid of the basket and saw the beautiful sleeping child inside. He awoke, gazed up in fright, and began to cry.

"What a lovely baby!" said the Princess, her kind heart filled with pity. "Let me hold you. Don't cry any more."

She lifted the baby from his little boat and rocked him gently.

He heard her kind voice and stopped crying. Then he smiled, and the Princess lost her heart to him.

"This must be one of the babies who were meant to be thrown into the river Nile," said the Princess. "It is a child of one of the slaves. I wish he were mine. He is so beautiful."

She could not bear to think he might be thrown into the river and drowned.

Miriam was still watching from her hiding place. She had held her breath when the maid fetched the ark. Then how glad she was to see the Princess take up the baby and nurse him so lovingly!

The little girl crept out of her hiding place. She stood looking shyly at the Princess. The Princess saw her and smiled.

"Do you want a nurse for the baby?" asked Miriam anxiously. "Shall I fetch one of the slaves for you? I know one who could nurse him."

The Princess looked down at the baby and made up her mind to keep him. "Go," she said to Miriam. "Bring me someone to nurse this child and love him."

Miriam ran home and rushed to her mother. Jochabed looked up, her face still stained with tears. "What is it?" she asked. "What news have you of our baby?"

"Good news, Mother!" said Miriam, joyfully. "The Princess came to bathe and she found our little baby. She said she wished he were her own."

"Will he be safe then?" asked Jochabed joyfully.

"Yes, he will," said Miriam, "and, oh, Mother, the Princess wants a nurse for him. You must come."

Jochabed hurried to the waterside with Miriam. She saw the Princess there, the baby still in her arms.

Jochabed spoke humbly. "You want a nurse for the child, great Princess?"

The Princess looked up and smiled. "Yes," she said. "I have found this beautiful baby floating in an ark on the water. I want a nurse for him because when he is old enough I shall make him my own son. Will you take him and look after him for me until he has grown into a fine boy?"

Jochabed could hardly speak for joy. She held out her arms for the baby. The Princess put him into them and the child smiled. He knew his mother.

Then the Princess guessed that Jochabed was really his mother, and she knew that he would be well cared for and loved. "Look after him well," she said. "I will pay you wages, and, when the time comes, you shall bring him to me, and he shall live with me, and be like a little prince."

Jochabed took her baby away, rejoicing. Miriam went with her, very happy too. Now their baby would not be taken away and drowned; he would belong to them, and grow up with them.

"You will not need to hide him any more, Mother," said Miriam. "The Princess will not allow the soldiers to harm him."

So no longer was the baby hidden away but lived happily with his family, growing stronger and bigger every month.

The Princess did not forget the baby she had taken from the waters. She thought of him often, and made plans for the day when the child should come to the palace.

The baby grew well. Soon he was old enough to leave his mother and go to the Princess.

One day his mother took him to the palace. She said goodbye to him, for now he must dress as an Egyptian, learn the ways of the overlords, and forget that he was the son of a slave.

The Princess was proud of the beautiful boy. She drew him to her lovingly.

"I shall call you 'Moses,'" she said. "That means 'Taken from the water,' little son."

And so the boy was known as Moses, the child taken from the waters. He was brought up as a prince, and wore fine clothes and ate good food. He was taught many things and grew up into a strong and wise youth.

But he never forgot that he was the son of a slave, and he pitied his people as he saw them toiling day by day in the hot sun.

"One day," he thought, "I will rescue them. I will be their leader, and they shall follow me."